Francis Takes a Tumble
The Story of the Good Samaritan

Written and Illustrated by
Damon J. Taylor

Kidzone

FOR PARENTS
with Dr. Sock

This story will help children understand that God wants us to love others—even if others don't love us.

Read It Together–

The story of the Good Samaritan is found in the New Testament book of Luke, chapter 10.

Sharing–

Tell your child about a time you went out of your way to help a stranger or someone you hardly knew.

Discussion Starters–

• Do you know a bully, or are you bothered by someone who doesn't like you?

• Is there a person you don't really like? Why don't you like him or her?

• Why did the two kids run off and leave Francis lying hurt on the playground?

• Why did Jesus tell the story of the Good Samaritan?

• In the story of the Good Samaritan, which person would you be—the priest, the second stranger, or the Samaritan?

For Fun–

Go with your kids on a mission to find someone to help. Hold a door for a man. Help a frazzled mom with her groceries. Let a person go ahead of you in line at the store.

Draw–

Draw with your kids. Each of you draw a picture of yourself being helpful to someone.

Prayer Time–

After reading the story, pray with your kids. Ask God to help each of you to see those in need and to help them.

COLEMAN HAS FOUND THAT THE LIFE OF A LITTLE BOY

can be tough at times, especially if that boy has a baby sister named Shelby. When Shelby was born, Coleman needed a way to deal with his day-to-day problems. He found his socks. Yes, that's right, his socks.

It may seem weird, but these aren't your regular, everyday tube socks that you find in your dresser. As ordinary as they may appear, these socks really are Coleman's friends, and they help him with his problems. When life gets complicated, Coleman goes to his bedroom and works through his troubles by playing make-believe with his socks and remembering Bible stories he's learned.

So please sit back, take off your shoes and socks if you like, and enjoy Coleman's imaginary world in . . .

francis Takes a Tumble
*The Story of the
Good Samaritan*

It was just another day at the playground. The birds were singing, Coleman was playing with his sock buddies, and…

...Francis was being mean to kids who were on the jungle gym. Francis is the playground bully.

He liked to climb to the top of the jungle gym and keep other kids from playing on it.

"I am king of the playground!" shouted Francis as he pushed the other kids off the jungle gym. "I am king of the world!"

Francis' foot suddenly slipped off the bar. "All must bow down . . . to MEEEEEE!!" he yelled as his hands lost their grip.

Francis hit the ground with a THUD!

Francis was hurt.
The kids at the
jungle gym made
excuses not to help
Francis.

"I think I hear my mom calling me," said Rachel and she ran off.

"I'd help," said Lee, "but these are my new clothes. I don't want to get them dirty."

Coleman saw Francis fall down. He saw the other kids run off and not help. He knew Francis was hurt, but he didn't budge from the bench.

"Coleman Riley Taylor, you should be ashamed of yourself!" said Sockariah, Coleman's imaginary sock buddy. "Go and help Francis. He may really be hurt!"

"Help him?!" said Coleman. "I'll bet he's fine. He's just waiting for someone to come close so he can punch him. Besides, he hates me!"

"You know," said Sockariah, "this reminds me of a story in the Bible. . . ."

A man once asked Jesus, "What do I need to do to get to heaven?"

Jesus asked him, "What does the law say?"

He replied, "I am to love the Lord with all of my heart, soul, strength, and mind. And I am to love my neighbor as much as I love myself. But . . . who is my neighbor?"

Jesus told the man a story that went like this. . . .

A Jewish man was walking down a road from Jerusalem to Jericho. Along the way, three bandits were hiding behind a rock. They were waiting to attack the next person who walked by.

The bandits beat the man and took his money. Then they left him lying beside the road. The man was injured and nearly dead.

A short time later, a priest came along. He noticed the injured man by the road. Instead of stopping to help the man, the priest kept walking down the road. The priest thought, "Boy, am I glad that didn't happen to me. I must hurry on my way. I think I hear my mother calling."

A little while later, another stranger passed by. He saw the injured man lying by the road. He thought, "This guy is in bad shape. I'd help, but these are new clothes. I don't want to get them dirty.

I'm sure someone else will come along and help this poor man."

And the second stranger left the injured man lying by the road.

At last, a Samaritan man came riding by and saw the injured Jewish man.

Now, the Samaritans and the Jews did not like each other. But this Samaritan knew what God wanted him to do.

The Samaritan bandaged the man's cuts. Then he put him on his donkey and took him to an inn so that he could get well.

He left the injured man at the inn. He gave the innkeeper extra money to help the man get better.

"So Coleman, what did you learn from all this?" asked Sockariah.

"Well, I learned that I'm not the only kid at the playground who is afraid of Francis," said Coleman.

"And…?" asked Sockariah.

"And I learned that even though Francis and I don't like each other, God wants me to do the right thing." Coleman hopped off the bench. "I'm going to help Francis."

"That's a good idea, Coleman. A really good idea."

The Child Sockology Series

For ages up to 5

Baby Boy, Bundle of Joy
Bible Babies
Bible Characters A to Z
Bible Numbers 1 to 10
Bible Opposites
New Testament Bible Feelings
Old Testament Bible Feelings
Times We Pray

For ages 5 and up

A Little Man with a Big Plan: The Story of Young David
The Ark and the Park: The Story of Noah
Beauty and the Booster: The Story of Esther
Forgive and Forget: The Story of Joseph
Francis Takes a Tumble: The Story of the Good Samaritan
Hide and Sink: The Story of Jonah
Lunchtime Life Change: The Story of Zacchaeus
To Cheese or Not To Cheese: The Story of Ruth